Secret Agent Splat

D0537480

Rob Scotton

HarperCollins *Children's Books*

Splat's dad makes toy ducks,
all colours, all sizes.
He makes lots of ducks.

The ducks are kept in the garden shed and
Splat has names for each and every one.

John

Paul

Ringo

George

One day Splat was shocked to see that the red duck was missing!

"Who messed with my ducks?"
asked Splat. Seymour shrugged.

The next day, the blue duck was missing and the red duck was back . . . but without a beak!

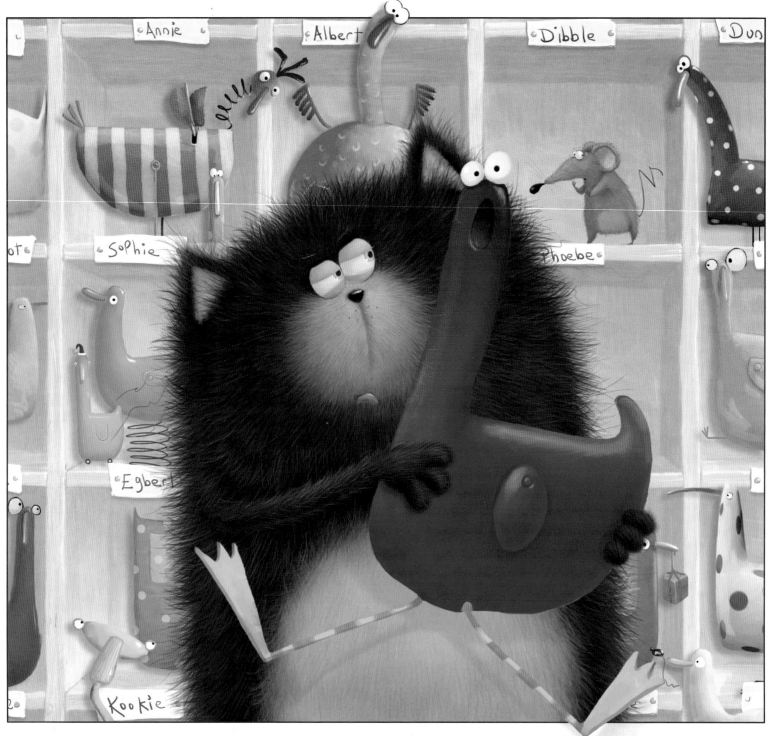

"Who messed with my ducks?" asked Splat.
Seymour shrugged.

The day after that, the green duck was missing
and the blue duck was back. Again, without a beak!

It was time to investigate.

"Who messed with my ducks?" asked Splat.
"Not me," said his mum.

"Not me," said Little Sis.

"Not me," said his brother.

"It seems that no one has messed with my ducks.
Not anyone. Not anybody. Nobody," said Splat.
"I must find this Mr Nobody!"

Splat watched his favourite TV show and made his plans.

"If my plan is to work," said Splat, "I must be clever, cunning and quick."

"I will find Mr Nobody and solve the mystery of the missing ducks."

"This is a job for. . .

Seymour, code named S, gave him his spy kit:
a camera, some flour, a torch, a book of paw prints
and a top-secret gizmo.

Secret Agent Splat put his plan into action.

He set his traps. . .

. . .and waited.

It was quiet. Too quiet!

Suddenly, there was a flash of light.

Secret Agent Splat raced to the scene.

His trap had been sprung. The camera had taken a photo.

Splat looked closely at the photo.

"Aha, ears!" exclaimed Splat. "Hmm, very familiar ears."

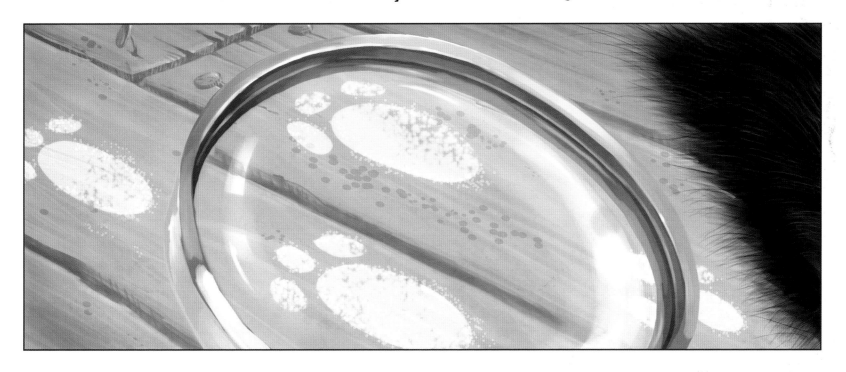

Splat looked at the flour he had sprinkled on the floor.
"Aha, paw prints!" exclaimed Splat. "Hmm, very familiar paw prints."

Splat followed the paw prints
from his shed. . .

. . .along a track to another shed.
"Mr Nobody's hideout," whispered Splat.

Splat tiptoed up to the door and pulled out his top-secret gizmo.

He pressed the latch, flung the door open...

Bright yellow eyes stared from the shadows.

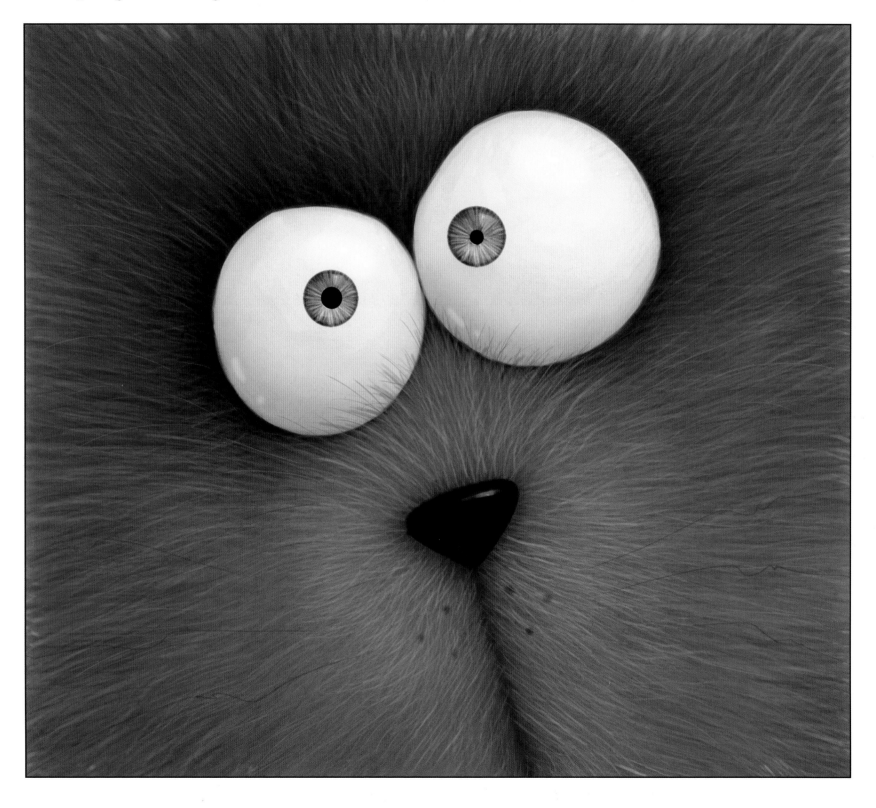

"So, Secret Agent Splat, you found me!" replied a mysterious voice.

"Aha! A mysterious voice," thought Splat.
"Hmm, a very familiar mysterious voice."

Splat shone his torch. He gasped. It was Spike!
"Spike! So you're Mr Nobody!"

Spike turned to run.

Splat pressed a button and released his top-secret gizmo.

Boing!

went the gizmo and
Spike fell to the floor.

Splat sat on him.

"Why, Spike?" Splat asked. "Why did you mess with my ducks?"

At that moment, a mouse ran past carrying another duck.
"That's strange," said Splat.

"Aw!" Spike said. "Not another one!"

The mouse ran into a small hole.
With a *thunk*, the duck's beak was knocked off as it struck the wall.

"Aw!
Not
another
bill!"

Splat looked into the hole.

The mouse was having a cup of tea with the duck.
"I asked Mouse not to take the ducks, but he didn't listen," said Spike.
"And since I don't want him to get in trouble, I've been returning the ducks."

"Now I see," said Splat. "But why did Mouse take my ducks?"

Splat thought for a while. "Hmm, maybe it's not really a duck that he wants," said Splat.

Splat whispered to Seymour. Seymour nodded.

"Maybe it's a friend!"

The Case of the Missing Ducks was solved.